To Taylor & Kai from Grandma G. J

When Glory Got Her Glow Back

When Glory Got Her Glow Back

A Glowworm's Tale

Laurel Lund

Illustrations by Alicia Newcomb

Balboa Press books may be ordered through booksellers or by contacting:

Balboa Press
A Division of Hay House
1663 Liberty Drive
Bloomington, IN 47403
www.balboapress.com
1-(877) 407-4847

Printed in the United States of America

ISBN: 978-1-4525-6011-3 (sc)
ISBN: 978-1-4525-6012-0 (e)

Library of Congress Control Number: 2012918290

Balboa Press rev. date: 10/26/2012

BALBOA
PRESS
A DIVISION OF HAY HOUSE

To my mother and father, who always taught us to shine.

The day began like any other day.
Except when it did not.
Today was that day.

Glory the Glowworm awakened from her sweet slumber on an elderberry bark leaf, stretched and greeted the morning as she always did, like a child who is curious and fun to be with.

Before beginning her day, she inched her way to the nearby spring to freshen her face. As she peered into the cool, clear water, she noticed something odd. Her image, reflected in the water, was not shining. Her magnificent aura, that light that shone around her like a beautiful blanket of color, had dimmed.

Glory's glow did not glow.

Where did her glow go? She had to know. So she set out on a mission, a journey to help Glory get her glow back.

It was early morning when she set out on her travels. Glory had so little time. She needed to get back home before dark in case she could not find her glow to light the way home. She carefully inched her way past the spring to the most beautiful garden whose sights and smells made her want to dance, *if only she had feet!* There, pacing up and down on a finely turned flower stem, was a very prim and proper creature in a red polka dot coat.

"Good morning," Glory said to a very ladylike Ladybug. "My name is Glory, and I am looking for my glow. Have you seen it anywhere?"

"No," answered the Ladybug, "but I might give you a clue. The color of my coat is red, and red represents the Life Force. It is the energy that keeps you alive, like a battery that recharges you at play or an engine that revs up your motor at school. **Red** is the color I HAVE. When you have the color red, you have everything you need to live life to the fullest. To live life to the fullest, simply live in the moment, not in the past or the future but in the now. For in life, the "wow" is in the now.

"I cannot lend you my coat, but I can share its red color to give you new life on your journey. Just close your eyes, imagine the color red and breathe it in deeply. Fill yourself full with it. Full-fill yourself."

Glory breathed in the color red until it seemed to fill every cell in her body. After a minute or three she began to feel a little tingle below her tummy. Curious, she looked down in time to behold a bright red ball of light right in that very spot.

Surprised and pleased, she felt energized knowing she had everything she needed to help search for her glow.

And so Glory wandered on through the grass, passing broken twigs and small stones and even a slippery snail that was even slower than she was. Suddenly, a slight breeze stirred above her head, and she looked up to see a flutter of butterflies in all colors of the rainbow. But one butterfly truly caught her eye: a magnificent Monarch whose gauzy orange wings had created the breeze that tickled Glory's nose and made her giggle.

Between giggles, Glory introduced herself to the Monarch and explained that she was in search of her glow. "Can you help me find my glow?" she asked.

"Of course, I can help," fluttered the butterfly, radiant in her glamorous orange gown. "**Orange** is the color I CREATE. To find your glow, you need to be creative. Without the color orange, you could never solve problems or make the world a better place. You are a co-Creator with the Universe. What you think and feel is what you create because thoughts are things. They are real. Where your attention goes, your energy flows.

"To take a bit of creativity with you on your journey, simply close your eyes, imagine the color orange and breathe it in deeply. Fill yourself full with it. Full-fill yourself."

As Glory imagined herself bathed in orange, she was overcome with happiness, for orange is also the color of emotion, whether happy or sad, mad or glad.

She giggled again because along with her happiness came a warmth just above the red in her tummy. She looked down and, to her surprise, noticed the spot turning orange. It delighted her and put a little wiggle in her walk, a sashay in her step. Glory was feeling happy to be creating her own future as she continued to inch her way toward it.

Glory thanked the magical Monarch and, still giggling, continued on her journey. The garden was situated on the edge of a cornfield with its stately green and yellow stalks. It led to a barnyard with a flock of ducklings, a gaggle of geese and a goat or two or three. Standing over them was a frightening creature that looked like a mean man with straw sticking wildly from its hands and legs. Startled, Glory jumped back and gasped. Her eyes were wide with fear.

But a tiny yellow Duckling at the scarecrow's feet said, "Do not be afraid. Fear only comes from feeling you have no power. I am the color yellow, the color of empowerment, of believing in yourself, like the confidence you have when you get an A on a report card or kick the winning soccer goal.

"To find your glow, you need to believe in your own power. Yellow is the color I CAN. You can do anything when you believe in yourself. For what you believe, you receive."

"I believe, I believe," cried Glory. "But how can I be certain I always will?"

"Simply close your eyes," said the Duckling. "Imagine the color yellow, the color of my coat, and breathe it in deeply. Fill yourself full with it. Full-fill yourself."

As Glory breathed in the color yellow, she felt a tingling just above her tummy, as if it was surrounded by a warm yellow light. And, indeed, she was! As she breathed in the color yellow, the spot above her tummy also turned yellow.

She smiled, thanked the little Duckling and again continued on her journey. But before she inched out of sight, she heard the little creature whisper: "It is good to believe in your own power, but remember that your true power is in your softness, in your gentleness."

It was nearing noon, and the sun was high in the sky. *At least IT still glowed, Glory thought.* And it was glowing brightly, reflected in a small pond just beyond the barnyard. As Glory neared the edge of the pond, she heard a low, throaty croaking sound. She looked around for the sound and saw a large green Bullfrog over-proudly perched on a nearby lily pad.

Unimpressed with how impressed he was with himself, Glory introduced herself to what she considered a bellowing bully. "I am Glory the Glowworm," she said, "and I have lost my glow. Can you help me find it?"

"If I must help you, then I must," he croaked, his tongue darting out to catch a fly at lightning-quick speed. "You see, you are green, and I am green. And yet we are not the same. I am a handsome frog, and you are just a worm. But we are both creatures of the Universe, and so I suppose we are equally important. That is why I will help you find your glow.

"Green is the color I LOVE," the Bullfrog said, surprisingly. "To find your glow, you must learn to love yourself and others, even those who may not be like you. They may live in another neighborhood or play in a different playground. You must even learn to love the not-so-fun things that happen to you, like a skinned knee or a broken toy, because there are no accidents. Everything that happens to you is meant to happen to help guide you through the maze of life. That is because all your life you have been led, you are being led and you will continue to be led, just as you were led to me today.

"To know love, simply close your eyes, imagine the color green and breathe it in deeply. Fill yourself full with it. Full-fill yourself.

"Now revel in your greenness, and follow your heart," croaked the Bullfrog. "When you find it, you will glow."

Glory breathed in the color green and, as she did, she felt a tingling near her heart that was quickly turning into a bright green light. Glory was filled with loving thoughts, even toward the bellowing Bullfrog who was not a bully after all. *Always know what you're looking at, she thought, for things are not always as they seem.* As she continued on her journey, she was in love with the world and where it was leading her.

Glory felt lighthearted, as though she had a little skip to her step, which was impossible, of course, because "she knows no toes." As she was tap-tapping her imaginary happy feet, she heard a beautiful sound coming from on high. At first she could not find the source of the sound, but then she saw a flash of blue in the branches of a weeping willow tree at the edge of the pond. It was a glorious Bluebird sharing his sweet song, sharing his joy of just being a bluebird with all those who could hear.

"How handsome you are," said Glory, hoping the bird didn't like to snack on worms of the glowing kind. "What makes you so happy?" she asked. "If I am happy, will I find my glow?"

"Happiness is different for everyone," said the Bluebird. "For some, it means getting new toys. For others, it means earning a place on the honor roll. For still others, it may mean sharing secrets with a best friend. Once you know what makes you happy, you will want to share it with others. But be mindful of the words you use because thought directs energy. You create the life you have by what you say and think.

"My song shares my good thoughts with the world. That is why my coat is the color blue, the color of communication. Blue is the color I SPEAK."

"How can I, too, remember to think and speak good thoughts?" asked Glory.

"Simply close your eyes, imagine the beautiful blue color of my feathered jacket and breathe it in deeply. Fill yourself full with it. Full-fill yourself."

Glory did just that. As she did, her throat began to tingle as if her own beautiful song was beginning to make its way from her heart. The Bluebird smiled as he saw Glory's throat become ringed with bright blue light like a necklace of brilliantly lit sapphires. The beautiful color alone made Glory want to share her joy with the world, just as her little blue friend did.

"Thank you so much, kind bird," said Glory. *And thank you for not having me for lunch today, she thought,* as she inched her way to her next encounter.

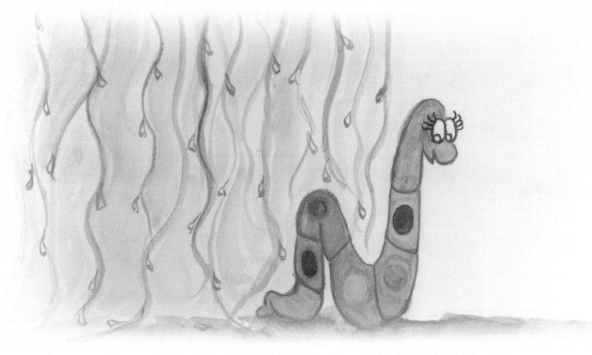

It was mid-afternoon, and Glory was amazed at the inner joy she felt as she inched along the edge of the pond. But she was also beginning to grow weary. She still had not found her glow. She was ready to rest for a moment when suddenly she found herself standing next to what appeared to be two very tall, very skinny trees. *Trees with feet!*

Confused, she gazed upward and realized she was not staring at a "forest of two" but at a stately bird standing in the water, wearing an eccentric-looking, indigo-colored feathered hat.

The oh-so-glamorous creature was so busy puffing up her chest and fluffing her feathers that she did not notice Glory in her pocket mirror. When she finally did, she apologized, saying, "You are so small that I did not see you. But I had a hunch you were coming to see me."

"Why?" asked Glory. "I myself did not even know I was coming here. Did my wonderful new friends tell you? You see, I am a glowworm who has lost her glow, and my new friends have been trying to help me get it back."

"No one told me," said the very exotic Egret. "I just knew because I am very intuitive. I listen to my inner voice, the one that tells me what I already know. And I pay attention to what I hear. That is why I have this very flattering, indigo-colored feathered hat. **Indigo** is the color I SEE. You should always follow what your inner self sees because your hunches are never wrong. And my hunch is that if you breathe in the color indigo and fill yourself full with it, full-fill yourself, you will soon get your glow back."

Hopeful, Glory took several deep breaths of indigo. As she did, it felt as though someone had turned on a bright indigo light right above her nose. When she looked into the big bird's mirror, she was, indeed, turning a bright indigo color, right smack between the eyes!

Glory's hunch was that the Egret's hunch was right. She may be close to finding her glow. But dusk was upon her, the sun was lower on the horizon and the stars were beginning to peek from the evening sky. She was discouraged. All sorts of colors swirled around her, but she still had not found her glow. And she must find it before dark or she would have no light to lead the way home. What was she to do? She leaned against one of the many flower stems near the pond and lowered her tiny head.

She began to sob. And sob. When she thought she had no more tears to cry, she became aware of a light breeze brushing her face, as if to dry her tears. She looked up to see a purple-throated Mountain-gem, a beautiful white hummingbird with a royal purple collar, who, between darting from flower to flower to gather her daily nectar, seemed to hover in place just above Glory's tear-stained face.

"You have traveled a long way to find your glow," said the lovely creature. "But do not be sad. I am here to help you. Come whisper your story in my ear. Tell me what you have learned on your journey."

"I have learned so many things," said Glory. "I have learned that life is a rainbow of colors and that each color has its own magical power. I have learned that:

- **Red** is the color I HAVE. It represents the Life Force. When you need pep in your step or the energy to proceed and succeed, living life to the fullest, breathe in the color red.

- **Orange** is the color I CREATE. It is the tint and tone of imagination and the emotions behind it. If you want to create a life filled with art, invention and ingenuity, breathe in the color orange.

- **Yellow** is the color I CAN. It is the symbol of confidence, of believing in yourself. When you need a boost of confidence or a sense of your own power, not power over others but power over yourself, breathe in the color yellow.

- **Green** is the color I LOVE. It represents appreciation of yourself and others. If you want to feel cherished, or if you need a hug, or if you want to give others a hug to let them know they are important, breathe in the color green.

- **Blue** is the color I SPEAK. It is the symbol of communication. When you want to create a life you love by willing only good thoughts and good words into your everyday work and play, breathe in the color blue.

- **Indigo** is the color I SEE. It is the sign of intuition, that inner voice that knows what you do not know you know. If you want to honor your hunches and act on them, for they are always right, breathe in the color indigo."

The humble Hummingbird literally hummed with approval. "You have learned much about yourself on this journey to get your glow back, little Glory. But it has really been a journey to find your Self. You are now surrounded by the colors of each lesson you learned along the way, every color of the rainbow. Almost. But you are still missing one color: purple.

"**Purple** is the color I KNOW. It is the symbol of harmony and unity. When you are surrounded by the color purple, you are connected to the Oneness of all things. You know that, like a snowflake, you are one of a kind. There is no one on Earth like you. You know that you are perfect, whole and complete as you are. You know who and what you are."

"I did learn who I am today," said Glory. "And I never want to forget. How can I make sure I remember?"

"Simply breathe in the color of my royal purple collar," said the Hummingbird, "and fill yourself full with it. Full-fill yourself."

Glory took in a deep, purple-tinted breath until she felt a tingling at the top of her head. At that instant, she was crowned with a rich purple light. Just as suddenly, with her entire body already lit up in swirls of brilliant colors, she felt another tingling, this time in her tail. As she turned to see what was happening, she grinned from ear to ear. Her tail was shining like a bright white light! Glory's glow did not go. She still had it! Glory had gotten her glow back!

"Glory be, it is me!" exclaimed the excited little glowworm. "How can that be?"

The Hummingbird hummed her answer. "You have found your balance, your tone, a vibration that is yours and yours alone. That is why you glow. Like a prism that breaks sunlight into all the colors of the rainbow, you also have all the colors of the rainbow inside you, whirling around like little wheels of energy. When you know who you are, and when all areas of your life are in harmony, you light up like a string of colored pearls. And all those colors blend together to become white light.

"It is not easy to find harmony in life. All sorts of things can throw you off balance. You may go down the wrong alley, take twists and turns, spin in a circle, fall off your bike or scrape your knee on the playground.

"But you will also have days that are right as rain, like the sound of two hands clapping, or hitting a home run or spending time with your best friend. When things are in balance, they just click into place. Doors just open, and you walk right through them.

"So even through life's bumps and bruises, stay focused on your goal, just as you did, and you will find balance. Your glow is a celebration of who you are. And the light it creates will take you all the way Home."

As Glory thanked her wise new friend and bid her farewell, she felt a newfound wisdom and freedom as she faced homeward, her taillight glowing like a beacon in the night, shining brightly to guide her and others who might follow. Because Glory had learned that once you know, you glow.

And like Glory, we are all meant to shine. Every one.

The Story Behind Glory's Story

Like Glory, you are a rainbow of color. You are a hue-man whose life force depends on spinning wheels of colorful energy called *chakras*.

Chakra (pronounced *chuhkruh*) is a Sanskrit word meaning *wheel* or *vortex*. The seven major chakras of the human body are nonphysical centers of spinning energy that enable you to generate and receive vibratory Life Force known as *chi* in China, *prana* in India and *mana* in Hawaii. Although these centers are nonphysical, they can be seen and measured by a process known as Kirlian photography.

These seven chakras are aligned in an ascending column along your spine from its base to the top of your head. Each chakra is located next to a specific hormonal gland and is governed by a different vibration. And each vibration is associated with a specific musical tone and color, which most cultures describe via the Rainbow System: **red** at the base of the spine, or root chakra; **orange** below the naval, or sacral chakra; **yellow** at the solar plexus chakra; **green** at the heart chakra; **blue** at the throat chakra; **indigo** at the brow, or third eye chakra; and **purple** or white at the crown chakra.

When all of your chakras are aligned and in balance, body-mind-spirit is in harmony. It is then that your life force, or aura, appears white. This was well known by early Christian artists, whose portraits of holy figures and saints were surrounded with a white halo called a *glory*.

The first known mention of chakras appeared in the ancient Hindu Upanishads around 200 BC. Similar mention can be found in the holy teachings of Tibetan Buddhism, Hinduism, Arabian Islam, early Christianity and the 5,000-year-old practice of traditional Chinese medicine. The concept of chakras was introduced to North American civilization by the Hopi Indians and was later introduced to Europe in the 1701 edition of the *Theosophia Practica,* a collection of letters written by German Bavarian mystic Johann Georg Gichtel.